The Magic School Bus Rides Again

Satellite Space Mission

by
AnnMarie Anderson

BRANCHES
SCHOLASTIC INC.

Ms. Frizzle's Class

Jyoti

Arnold

Ralphie

Wanda

Keesha

Dorothy Ann

Carlos

Tim

TABLE OF CONTENTS

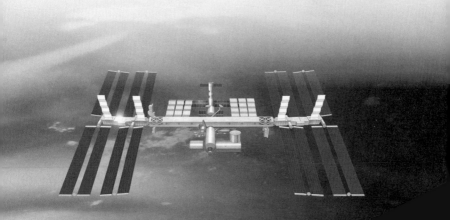

Published by Scholastic Inc., *Publishers since 1920*.
SCHOLASTIC, THE MAGIC SCHOOL BUS, BRANCHES, and logos are trademarks
and/or registered trademarks of Scholastic Inc. All rights reserved.

Library of Congress Cataloging-in-Publication Data available

ISBN 978-1-338-26429-6 (hardcover) / ISBN 978-1-338-26251-3 (paperback)

10 9 8 7 6 5 4 3 2 1   18 19 20 21 22
Printed in China   38

First edition, August 2018
Edited by Marisa Polansky
Book design by Jessica Meltzer

CHAPTER 1

SOCCER SLIP-UP

Ms. Frizzle's class was just one point away from a win in their big soccer game. Keesha was in goal, and Jyoti was playing defense. The soccer ball soared toward the net.

"Keesha!" Jyoti shouted. "Keesha! Heads up!"

But Keesha wasn't paying attention to the game. She was staring at the papers in her hand. Jyoti jumped in the air and knocked the ball away from the goal with a roundhouse kick.

The crowd cheered.

"What a save!" Wanda yelled into her announcer's microphone. "But not by the Walkerville Wildcat goalie. It looks like she's distracted by . . . paperwork?" Keesha was staring at a piece of paper instead of staring at the ball.

"Thanks, Jyoti," Keesha said. "I didn't even see that one coming!"

"No problem," Jyoti said.

Meanwhile, Carlos had the ball. He dribbled down the field and passed it to Dorothy Ann. Then Dorothy Ann kicked the ball to Ralphie, who launched it into the net. Goal!

The referee blew his whistle to end the game.

"The Walkerville Wildcats win!" Wanda shouted into the announcer's microphone. "That was some really amazing teamwork. They'll play again tomorrow for a shot at winning the Frizzle Cup, which will be broadcast around the world!"

The team gathered in the middle of the field. Ralphie high-fived Dorothy Ann.

"Great game!" Jyoti said.

Keesha turned to her teammates. "Sorry, guys," she told them. "I should have been paying attention back there. But I've been so distracted by my application to—"

"Astronaut camp!" everyone shouted.

"Oh, have I mentioned it already?" Keesha asked.

"Maybe once or twice . . ." Tim began.

". . . a minute . . ." Carlos chimed in.

". . . for the last week!" Ralphie finished.

"I know, I know," Keesha said. She shrugged. "But astronaut camp is my ticket to my dream—a career in space!"

"And a distracted goalie is *our* ticket to defeat!" Ralphie groaned. The team had to win the next game to move on to the finals.

"Don't worry," Jyoti said. "Keesha will have her head in the game tomorrow, I promise."

"Really?" Dorothy Ann asked. "How?"

"I'm going to help her finish her astronaut camp application!" Jyoti said proudly. She was a whiz with technology and she had a great idea of how she could help Keesha earn a spot in camp.

"Okay," Keesha agreed, "but it won't be easy. I still need something extra special. Something that really shows them how great I would be in space."

"How about a selfie—in space?" Jyoti asked.

"Huh?" Wanda asked. "How are you going to do that?"

"You'll see," said Jyoti.

CHAPTER 2

LIFTOFF!

Jyoti and Keesha were waiting for science class to start when Jyoti pulled out her tablet and launched her photo app.

"This will make it look like you were in space. Which planets or stars do you want in the background?" Jyoti asked as she swiped through the app's choices.

"Hmm. I don't know," Keesha said. Before she could say another word, the class was interrupted. In walked their teacher, Ms. Fiona Frizzle. She was wearing a space suit and bouncing a soccer ball on her knee.

Ms. Frizzle removed her helmet. She had just returned from space. "Nothing like playing soccer in zero **gravity** to get the blood pumping! I just kicked the ball through Saturn's rings!"

Suddenly, Wanda burst through the door, looking worried.

"Ms. Frizzle!" she cried. "We have a problem!"

If someone—or something—needed saving, Wanda was going to be the one to help.

"Okay, Wanda, shoot!" Ms. Frizzle replied with a chuckle. "Did you get my soccer joke? I crack myself up!"

"It's the FrizTV broadcast network," Wanda cried. "The whole network is off the air!"

"The FrizCast is on the fritz?" Ms. Frizzle asked.

Wanda nodded. "That means there will be kids all over the world who can't watch the Frizzle Cup games this afternoon."

"That sounds like a problem with a FrizNet satellite," Ms. Frizzle replied.

"Satellite?" Ralphie asked. "What's that?"

Dorothy Ann prided herself on having an answer for everything.

"Satellites are objects that have been put in Earth's **orbit** for some reason," she explained. "In this case, they're used for broadcasting soccer games."

"That's right!" Ms. Frizzle agreed. "My network of FrizSats is in orbit all around the globe. Sounds like we should go up there and see what's going on."

"Up there?" Keesha asked excitedly. "You mean *to space*?"

"You got it, Keesha!" said Ms. Frizzle.

"Yes!" Keesha pumped her fist. "Well, what are we waiting for? Let's get to the bus!"

"I couldn't have said it better myself," Ms. Frizzle agreed.

Ms. Frizzle was definitely not an average teacher. She loved taking her students on unbelievable field trips on her Magic School Bus. And this time, it looked like they were going to outer space! The class ran out of the classroom and headed to the bus.

"This is so perfect, Jyoti!" Keesha said. "Now I can actually take a picture in space instead of just using the app!"

Jyoti frowned. "But I thought we were going to check the satellites so we can get the game broadcast working," she said.

"Of course," Keesha said. "But we can also take *my* picture—in space!"

"Here we go, kids," Ms. Frizzle said. "Prepare your pressure suits. Soon we'll have liftoff!"

Arnold groaned and pulled his seat belt as tight as it would go. Arnold preferred learning in the classroom to flying through space in a magic bus. "Maybe I should have stayed home today," he groaned.

"Don't worry, Arnold. According to my calculations, we'll be perfectly safe," said Dorothy Ann.

As Dorothy Ann spoke, the school bus magically transformed into a rocket.

"Hang on, kids," Ms. Frizzle warned. "We're going for a ride!"

"Yay!" the class cried. "A field trip!"

"Three . . . two . . . one . . . liftoff!" Ms. Frizzle shouted as the bus blasted through a layer of clouds.

"Amazing!" Carlos said as he peered out the window. "Where are we going?"

"Straight up," Wanda replied with a laugh.

"Not for long," Keesha corrected her as the bus rocket **accelerated** through the clouds and made an arc.

"Whoa," Carlos said to Keesha, impressed. "How did you know that?"

"If you want to go to astronaut camp, you have to know these things," Keesha said.

The kids pressed their faces to the window as the blue sky faded into black space dotted with millions of twinkling stars.

"No way!" Dorothy Ann cried breathlessly. "More stars than you can count!"

"So awesome," Ralphie said.

"Are we in orbit yet, Ms. Frizzle?" Keesha asked.

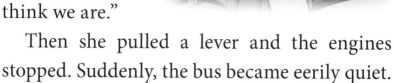

"Yes, Keesha," the Friz replied. "I think we are."

Then she pulled a lever and the engines stopped. Suddenly, the bus became eerily quiet.

"Turn it back on!" Arnold cried. "What's wrong? Why did you stop the engines?"

CHAPTER 3

ORBIT EXPERTS

The kids began to float out of their seats. Ralphie's hat flew off his head and tumbled through the air.

"What's going on?" Arnold gasped.

"We're in space!" Keesha cheered.

"That's right, Keesha," the Friz replied. "We are now in low orbit around Earth."

"What does *that* mean?" Arnold groaned.

"It means now that the bus is at the right speed and height above Earth, we don't need the engines anymore," Ralphie explained as they floated out of their seats. "There's barely any **atmosphere** to slow us down, so we can just coast in orbit."

"Yeah, well, I'm not taking any chances," Arnold said. He made his way back to his seat and buckled his seat belt.

"What are you doing, Arnold?" Jyoti asked, confused.

"No engines!" Arnold replied frantically. "That means any second now we could fall back down to our doom!"

"Not quite, Arnold," Ms. Frizzle said. "Being in orbit is a perfect balance. We're circling at a speed that's just fast enough to resist Earth's gravity. If we went too slow, we would be pulled down."

"But if we sped up too much, we would fly off into space!" Keesha said, pointing to the projection screen on the bus. She had been studying space a *lot* to prepare for astronaut camp.

"Explain it all you want," Arnold replied. "I'm not taking off my seat belt until we get home."

"Hey!" Jyoti yelled, pointing out the window at a huge piece of equipment floating by. "I think I just spotted a satellite!"

"Good eye, Jyoti," Ms. Frizzle said. "Buckle up, kids. It's time to get to a higher orbit!"

As the kids tightened their seat belts, Ms. Frizzle fired up the rocket boosters.

"Wait!" Keesha gasped suddenly. "Stop—now!"

The Friz put on the brakes and stopped the bus.

"What is it?" Wanda asked.

"You'll see in a second," Keesha said. "Jyoti, grab my camera. Quick!"

Arnold stayed put. The rest of the class unbuckled their belts and floated toward Keesha. Jyoti grabbed the camera. Keesha pointed out the window and down toward Earth.

"Look down there," she said with a squeal. "It's the *exact* place where they hold astronaut camp! It's perfect for my application."

She posed for the camera.

"Okay, Jyoti," Keesha continued. "I'm ready for my close-up! Space cheese!"

"You stopped us for *that*?" Tim asked.

But before Keesha could reply, something hit the bus with a giant *thud*. The kids bounced around the bus like soccer balls in a net.

"Ahhhh!" they shouted as they bumped into one another.

"Wh-wh-what was that?" Arnold gasped.

CHAPTER 4

JUNK IN SPACE

Space junk!" Ms. Frizzle cried. "I've always wondered what would happen if it hit us, and now I know—"

"That it's bad!" Arnold interrupted.

Ms. Frizzle pushed a few buttons on the dashboard as an alarm sounded.

Beep! Beep! Beep!

"What's happening?" Carlos asked. He floated to the front of the bus.

The kids gathered around Ms. Frizzle as she swiped through some screens on the bus's computer.

"Okay, so apparently that space junk knocked out power to our engines," Ms. Frizzle explained. Then she glanced out the window and noticed another incoming piece of junk.

"Hang on, kids. We're about to go for a spin!"

Suddenly, there was another jolt, and the bus began to free-fall.

"Whoaaaaa!" the kids cried as they flew around inside the bus.

"Guys, I'm so sorry!" Keesha shouted.

"Are you kidding me?" Ralphie replied. "This is a blast!"

"Yeah," Wanda agreed. "We're flying!"

The bus slowed down.

"What is space junk anyway?" Ralphie asked.

Dorothy Ann pulled out her tablet and tapped away.

"According to my research, it's machine parts and waste that's left over in space from old satellites and rockets," she explained. "There are thousands of pieces going around Earth all the time."

BAM!

Another piece of junk slammed into the bus and sent them spinning in the other direction.

"Ahhhh!" the kids cried as they bounced around again.

"I can't believe D.A.'s doing research while we're getting pounded by space garbage!" Ralphie cried.

Suddenly, Wanda noticed something outside.

"Hey, look out the window, you guys," she said.

"It's a satellite!" Keesha cried.

"And there's way more space junk, too," Carlos added as he pointed to the other objects floating past the bus.

"Great gawking, kids," Ms. Frizzle said as she floated over to them. "And who needs engine power anyway? That space junk gave us a big push into a higher orbit! Now keep your eyes peeled for a Friz communications satellite. It beams pictures, sound waves, radio waves—and soccer games!"

"You mean like that one?" Dorothy Ann asked. She pointed to a satellite with an image of the Magic School Bus on it.

"That's it!" Ms. Frizzle said as the bus moved closer to the satellite. "Amazing, isn't it?"

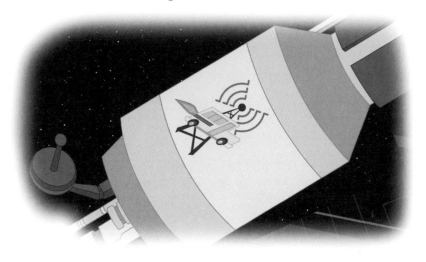

Ms. Frizzle popped up a video screen with a diagram that showed how a satellite works.

"When a ground station on Earth sends information up, the satellite acts like a mirror and bounces the signal back down to another ground station," Ms. Frizzle explained.

"Like passing a soccer ball!" Ralphie said.

"Look!" Dorothy Ann exclaimed as she pointed to the screen. "The signal goes in a straight line, so it needs to bounce from satellite to satellite to get around the curve of the Earth."

"So that's how we send a live stream of our soccer game to the other side of the world?" Tim asked. "Cool!"

"Yup," Ms. Frizzle agreed. "Now, to fix the satellite, we have to take space pods to get to it. And by 'we,' I mean 'you'!"

"Space pods?" the kids cried. "Awesome!"

"Uh-uh." Arnold shook his head. "I am *not* going. I'm allergic to space pods!" he joked.

CHAPTER 5

SLOW UNTIL YOU KNOW

Ms. Frizzle floated to the back of the bus and entered a code on a keypad. A secret door slid open to reveal a row of brand-new bright-yellow space pods.

"Cool!" the kids cried.

"Now, they take some getting used to," Ms. Frizzle explained, "so go slow until you know how to handle it. And there's one thing to keep in mind . . ."

But Keesha wasn't listening. She was looking out the window.

"This is the perfect spot for my picture!" she whispered.

Meanwhile, Ms. Frizzle was giving the class important instructions.

"See this glowing button?" She pointed to a special button on the space pod. "Now, listen carefully . . ."

But Keesha was busy daydreaming.

I wonder what astronaut camp will be like, she thought. *Maybe I'll get to meet super-famous astronaut Kathy K. Kuiper!*

Keesha squealed out loud in excitement just thinking about it.

"So whatever you do, don't push the button!" Ms. Frizzle warned.

"Got it!" replied everyone except Keesha. She hadn't heard a word of Ms. Frizzle's instructions.

Arnold nervously climbed into a space pod, and the other kids followed. They put on special headsets that allowed them to talk to Ms. Frizzle—and one another. Then they drove their pods out of the bus and into space.

"Let's do a total system check of the satellite," Jyoti said as she moved her pod closer to the broken device.

"No physical damage that I can see," Wanda said as she floated around to the other side of the satellite.

"All the blinky lights look nice and blinky!" Tim confirmed.

Jyoti noticed that Keesha's pod was far away from the rest of the class.

"Keesha!" she called. "We could use your help over here. What are you doing?"

"I'm getting an even better photo for my application," Keesha replied. "This is the perfect spot!"

Keesha pulled a lever and stepped on the gas to make her pod move forward. But instead, she flipped upside down.

"Whoa!" Keesha cried. She steadied the pod.

"Like the Friz said, go slow until you know!" Jyoti reminded her.

Keesha just shrugged.

"Don't worry, I can do this," she said confidently. "I'm practically an astronaut, remember?"

"Okay, but don't forget that the glowing button is—" Arnold began, but Keesha cut him off.

"Emergency stop," she said quickly. "Got it! Ohhhhh, that looks perfect over there. Bye-bye!"

Keesha zoomed off in her pod. She was determined to get the best photo possible for her application.

"Uh-oh," Arnold muttered.

"Did Keesha just says she thinks the glowing button means stop?" Jyoti asked.

"Yes," Tim groaned. "But it's really maximum zoom!"

Tim flew after Keesha, who was fiddling with her tablet and posing for her picture.

"Keesha, listen," Tim said through his headset. "This is import—"

"Tim!" Keesha cut him off. "You're in my picture."

She zoomed away from him.

Carlos tried next.

"Keesh, we just want to make sure—" Carlos began, but Keesha interrupted again.

"Ugh!" she groaned. "The sooner you all get out of the way, the sooner I'll get this picture!"

Keesha quickly pushed a few buttons, trying to move away from her friends so she could get the perfect shot. But instead, her space pod started spinning—fast!

"Ahhhhh!" she cried. "How do I stop this thing?"

"Uh-oh," Jyoti said nervously. "I just hope she doesn't push—"

"Maximum zoom!" the other kids all shouted.

But that is exactly what Keesha did.

CHAPTER 6

MAXIMUM ZOOM

Keesha's space pod zipped through space, picking up speed as it went.

"Congratulations!" a robotic voice inside the pod said. "You have reached maximum zoom! You are in low Earth orbit, passing the **International Space Station** and the **Hubble Telescope**. Now you're heading straight for a weather FrizSat."

"Oh, no!" Keesha cried as her space pod flew faster and faster. "I'm going to hit it!"

"Stand by for safety pillows," the voice continued.

"Safety pillows?!" Keesha gasped. "What are safety pillows?"

A second later, a **robotic arm** with a pillow on it smacked her in the face.

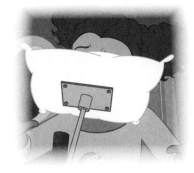

"Oof!" Keesha cried.

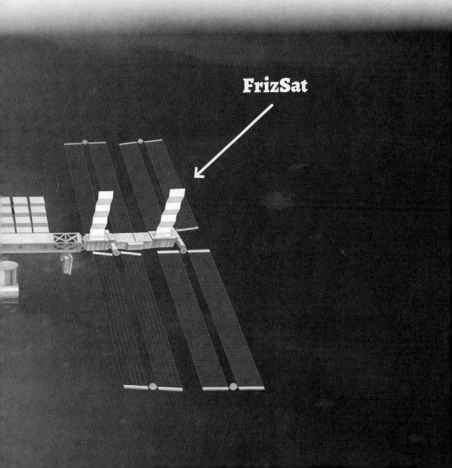

FrizSat

Then her space pod crashed into the satellite.
Wham!

The space pod whirled and twirled through space, bouncing from one satellite to the next.
Smash! Crash!

"You are now in medium Earth orbit," the computer continued.

"You're heading for a radio FrizSat."
Bang!

"Ahhhhh!" Keesha cried. "Help! I'm wrecking all the satellites!"

Keesha's space pod continued to bounce from one orbit to the next, knocking out satellite after satellite. Meanwhile, the other kids had flown their space pods back to the bus for help.

"Hang on, Keesha!" her friends cried.

Ms. Frizzle pressed a few buttons, and a robotic arm extended from the bus and grabbed Keesha's pod out of mid-space and scooping her back onto the bus.

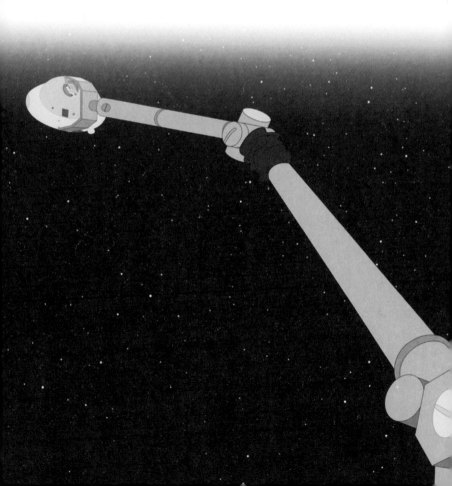

"So, the glowing button wasn't the emergency stop, huh?" Keesha asked. She looked down at the floor.

"Nope," Ms. Frizzle replied. "But the good news is that not many fifth graders have gone at maximum zoom through all of Earth's orbits. That's going to look great on your application!"

"You sure you're okay, Keesh?" Jyoti asked.

"I am," Keesha replied, "but I'm not sure about all those satellites!"

"Well, I am," the Friz said matter-of-factly. "The FrizSats were destroyed."

The kids groaned.

"All of them?" Tim asked.

"Yup," Ms. Frizzle replied. "I'm afraid every FrizSat in every orbit got knocked off its path."

"Let me guess," Dorothy Ann said as she tapped away on her tablet. "Not only is the soccer game satellite down, but so is everything else!"

"Not *everything* else," the Friz replied. "Just the Friz network!"

"What does that include?" Wanda asked.

"FrizComm, FrizWeb, FrizGPS, FrizRadio, Friz Weather Station, Friz Science Research, Friz Space Telescope, and FrizCat Videos." Ms. Frizzle rattled off the list with a shrug. "Other than that, we're all good!"

"Friz space is officially broken," Keesha cried. "And it's all my fault!"

CHAPTER 7

ASSEMBLY REQUIRED

Keesha floated over to Ms. Frizzle.

"Is there any way to fix those FrizSats?" she asked.

"They can't really be fixed," explained the Friz. "They'll need to be completely replaced."

The kids groaned again.

"According to my research, satellites take years to make and cost millions of dollars!" Dorothy Ann said as she pulled up a screen on her tablet. "What are we going to do?"

"Well, luckily I have a cousin in the satellite business," Ms. Frizzle replied, smiling.

"Really?" Ralphie asked. "No way!"

"Of course you do," Arnold joked.

Ms. Frizzle punched a few buttons on the dashboard and suddenly there was a delivery for  The Magic School Bus. Seven big boxes appeared for each student.

"Cool!" Carlos said as he grabbed a box and opened it up. Metal pieces, screws, and tools all floated out. "Huh? This doesn't look like a satellite."

"Well, there is some assembly required," said the Friz.

The kids quickly got to work building their satellites. Once the satellites were ready to go, the kids headed for the door.

"All right!" The Friz shooed them out of the bus. "You get out there and put the 'Friz' back in 'FrizSat'!"

"She means put the satellites back in orbit," Wanda explained. "I can stay on the bus and check out the links to make sure the satellites are working again."

"Got it!" Keesha replied. "Let's go!"

The other kids followed Keesha back out into space with their satellites. Once everything was in place, Keesha gave Wanda a thumbs-up through the window.

"Okay, everyone," Wanda instructed through her headset, "turn on your satellites!"

Keesha looked at hers nervously. The last time she had pressed a button, it hadn't gone so well. She took a deep breath.

"Here goes!" she said, pushing the green power button. A moment later, all of the lights on the satellite were blinking.

"Wanda," Keesha asked, "are the satellites communicating with Earth like they're supposed to?"

"Not yet," Wanda replied as she studied the computer screen. "Something's not right."

"Wait," Keesha said thoughtfully. "When the original FrizSats got smashed, they weren't just in one orbit. I zoomed all over the place!"

"How could we forget?" Ralphie joked.

"That means we have to find the right orbits for our new FrizSats," Keesha said.

"Yeah, but how do we do that?" Tim asked, puzzled.

"Well, what better way to find the right home for a satellite than to become a satellite?" the Friz asked.

"Oh boy," Arnold groaned. "I knew I should have stayed on Earth today!"

CHAPTER 8

FRIZSATS TO KIDSATS

A second later there was a flash of light, and the kids found themselves *inside* the machines they had just built.

"Wow!" Ralphie cried.

"This is so cool," Dorothy Ann marveled.

"But, Ms. Frizzle," Arnold asked, "how will we know when we're in the right orbit?"

"Trust me, Arnold," Ms. Frizzle said. "When you feel it, you'll know."

The kids zoomed through space in their satellites.

"So this is low Earth orbit," Tim said. "We're like two hundred miles away from Earth!"

"Yup!" Dorothy Ann agreed. Her satellite was nearby. "Or three hundred and forty kilometers."

Tim's satellite began to blink.

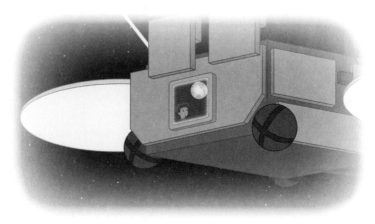

"Look!" Dorothy Ann said. "You're getting a signal."

"Cool!" Tim said as pictures of Earth popped up on his screen. "That explains why my cameras are pointed down."

"Awesome," Dorothy Ann replied. "My cameras are pointed the other way—out into space! I'm an astronomy satellite. Looks like I'm taking pictures of the universe and sending them to scientists back on Earth!"

Meanwhile, Jyoti, Arnold, and Carlos were in medium Earth orbit, about 12,500 miles—or 20,000 kilometers—above Earth.

"Hey, is anyone getting anything?" Jyoti asked.

Arnold's satellite crackled with static. Then a map appeared clearly on the screen.

"I am!" he said happily. "I'm a GPS FrizSat! I can help with maps and directions on Earth."

"Me, too!" Carlos shouted as a map appeared on his screen.

Finally, Jyoti's static cleared.

"Me three!" she cried. "Looks like we're working together as navigation satellites in medium Earth orbit."

"Great job!" Ms. Frizzle said from the bus.

"How's it going up in **geosynchronous** orbit, Ralphie?" Wanda asked as she scanned her computer screen. "You're currently in an orbit that matches Earth's rotation exactly!"

"It's great!" Ralphie said. His favorite pop song had just started playing. "I think I'm getting signals from a radio station on Earth."

"Looks like every satellite is in the right orbit. They all connect back to Earth with a strong signal," said Wanda.

"Excellent," said the Friz as she peered over Wanda's shoulder. "Is that everyone?"

"Almost," Wanda said as she studied her screen. "Everything on Earth is working except the video of the soccer game. So that must be Keesha! Keesha, are you there?"

"Yes!" Keesha replied. "Does that mean I'm not getting any signals?"

"It doesn't look like it," said Wanda from the bus.

"Oh, no," Keesha moaned. "Don't tell me I'm causing problems—again!"

CHAPTER 9

TEAM FRIZ

Keesha zoomed from low Earth orbit to medium Earth orbit to geosynchronous orbit and back again, but all she heard was static.

"I'm still not getting anything," Keesha reported. She was getting frustrated.

"Try going a little higher!" came Wanda's reply.

"Copy that," Keesha replied as she moved farther away from Earth. Suddenly, the static transformed into what sounded like a  cheering crowd of people. "Hey! I think I'm getting something!"

Back on the bus, an image of a goalie in a soccer net appeared on Wanda's tablet.

"The soccer broadcast!" Wanda shouted. "It's back online. You did it, Keesh!"

"This is so cool," Keesha said. "It's like I'm connected to the whole world!"

"Actually, you really are," Wanda explained. She pointed to the screen and pulled up an image of a communications signal zipping from a ground station on Earth to a FrizSat, to Keesha's satellite, and back to another ground station.

"There's a whole network of communication satellites working together, passing signals to one another—including you!"

"It's like we're all players in a gigantic game of space soccer!" Keesha giggled.

"That's exactly right!" said the Friz. "Mission accomplished! Now that the FrizSats are back in their spots, let's get all of you back, too!"

A few minutes later, the kids were back inside the bus.

"Nice pass!" Jyoti exclaimed as she watched the soccer game on the bus's big-screen TV.

"Thanks to all of you, the soccer game will be seen by everyone!" Ms. Frizzle said proudly.

Keesha cleared her throat.

"I'm sorry I wasn't a team player earlier, guys," she said. "After being a satellite, I get what it really means. It's so great to be connected and work together!"

"So I guess it's time for you to send in your astronaut camp application," Jyoti said. "Ready for your close-up?"

"Okay, I'll get out of the way," Ralphie said as he floated away.

"Oh, no," Keesha replied. She grabbed Ralphie's arm to stop him. Then she pulled Jyoti closer, too. "I want a picture of all of us—together. My team!"

"Thanks, Keesh!" Ralphie said.

Suddenly, the air lock door slid open and an unexpected guest floated into the bus. Keesha's jaw dropped open.

"Kathy K. Kuiper!" she gasped. "In person?
You're my favorite astronaut ever—eeeeeeek!"

Kathy gave the kids a friendly nod.

"Hi, everyone," she said. "I was just in the neighborhood, so I thought I'd drop in and see my old pal Fiona."

"Hi, Kathy!" the Friz replied warmly. "To what do we owe the pleasure?"

"Well, we're just opening up applications to astronaut camp," Kathy explained. "I thought you might have a recommendation. We're looking for someone who's a real team player."

Everyone turned to look at Keesha.

"I think we have just the person," Ms. Frizzle replied. "In the meantime, care to join us for a team photo?"

Ms. Frizzle held up her camera. "Say . . ."

"Space cheeeese!" the class shouted. Then, they huddled together for an out-of-this-world picture.

GLOSSARY

Accelerate: get faster and faster

Atmosphere: the mixture of gases that surrounds a planet

Geosynchronous: turning or rotating at the exact same time as Earth

Gravity: the force that pulls things down toward Earth and keeps them from floating away into space

Hubble Telescope: a telescope that orbits earth and helps scientists get a better view of outer space objects

International Space Station: a large spacecraft orbiting earth where astronauts live and work

Orbit: the invisible path followed by an object circling a planet or the sun

Robotic arm: a mechanical arm that works like a human arm to control tools or operate machines

Ask Professor Frizzle

What's up with all the trash in space? Why can't we keep space clean?

You can't make an omelet without breaking a few eggs, and we can't launch rockets into space without leaving behind some waste.

What kind of waste is left in space?

It's anything from loose screws to entire pieces of spaceships. And when there are collisions like Keesha's, the mess gets even messier.

Why didn't the bus rocket slow down when the Friz turned off the engines? It couldn't coast in orbit forever, could it?

 No. While there's much less air in the atmosphere in low Earth orbit than down on Earth, there is still enough to get in a spacecraft's way, slowing it down.

So eventually the bus rocket would fall?

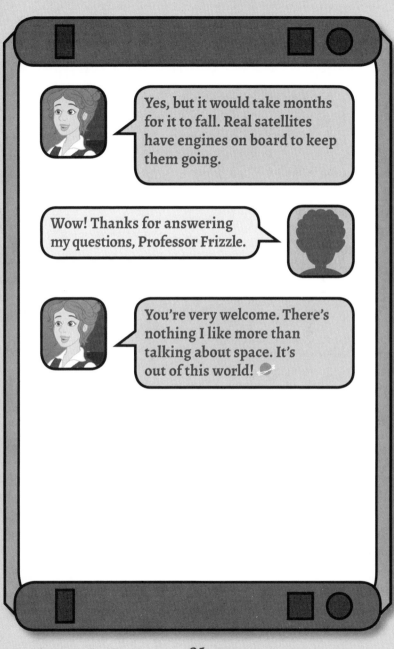

The Magic School Bus
Rides Again

QUESTIONS and ACTIVITIES

1. Keesha is so excited about applying to astronaut camp that she can't pay attention during the soccer game. If you could go to a specialty camp, what type of camp would it be?

2. If you could design your own satellite, what would it look like? Draw a picture.

3. The kids turned into satellites to learn more about how they work. If you could turn into any object to learn more about it, what would you choose and why?

4. How do you think Keesha's classmates felt when she wasn't being a team player?

5. What helped Keesha realize how important it was to work together with her friends?